RED FLOWER GOES WEST

ANN TURNER

ILLUSTRATED BY DENNIS NOLAN

HYPERION BOOKS FOR CHILDREN
NEW YORK

Copyright © 1999 by Ann Turner.
Illustrations © 1999 by Dennis Nolan.
All rights reserved. No part of this book may be reproduced or transmitted in any form or by any means,
electronic or mechanical, including photocopying, recording, or by any information storage and retrieval
system, without written permission from the publisher.
For information address Hyperion Books for Children,
114 Fifth Avenue, New York, New York 10011-5690.
Printed in Singapore.
First Edition
3 5 7 9 10 8 6 4 2
This book is printed in 21-point Centaur.
Designed by Christine Kettner.

Library of Congress Cataloging-in-Publication Data
Turner, Ann Warren.
Red flower goes west / by Ann Turner; illustrated by Dennis Nolan.—1st ed.
p. cm.
Summary: As they journey west, a family nurtures the red flower they have carried
with them from their old home.
ISBN 0-7868-0313-4 (trade)—ISBN 0-7868-2253-8 (lib. bdg.)
[1. Overland journeys to the Pacific—Fiction. 2. Flowers—Fiction.] I. Nolan, Dennis, ill. II. Title.
PZ7.T8535Rf 1998
[E]—dc21 98-11265

To my father,
who has gone on his last great journey
—A. T.

To my grandfather, Will Fortier,
who was born on the prairie on the way to California
—D. N.

There were no clouds in the sky
the day Pa said we were going west.
"There's gold in California and free land.
A man can't let that go by."
I looked at Jenny. She stared at me.
Once Pa had an idea, no one could stop him.
He sold our farm, sold our horses, Nat and Pat,
and got oxen. "Ugly!" Jenny turned away.

Ma tightened her lips, dug a red flower
from her garden, and set it in a wooden box.
"James, put this in the wagon." She handed it to me.
"Rachel! You're never taking that west!" Pa declared,
as he packed the wagon to bursting.
"Clem, you can ask me to leave my home and friends,
but this flower came from Mother's garden.
Where I go, this flower goes too."
Pa had nothing to say to that.

Ma started the journey with the flower on her lap.
I wished I had something to hold on to, too.
When we came to the Missouri,
Pa drove the oxen onto the ferry.
Jenny said, "I bet this is the first red flower
to cross this wide river.
She's a traveler, like us."
At night, when light from campfires shone
through our canvas top, I could see
Red Flower glowing warm and bright,
like a lantern to show us the way.

One day we came to a river so swift and rough
Pa stood on the bank, afraid. Others took
the ferry over, but we had no money for that.
"We'll just have to swim across." Pa tightened the top.
Water lapped the wagon bed, crept over my toes.
Pa jumped out to help the team.
We saw him go under the black surface and we screamed.
I clutched Red Flower, told her to watch over Pa,
then I saw an Indian dive in from the opposite bank.
When he came near the wagon he dove again and again
till he found Pa and his hat and held on to the oxen.
With his help, we made it to the opposite shore.

Shaking and wet, Pa came to by the fire,
and Ma tried to thank that brave Indian.
She held out Red Flower to him, but he smiled
and shook his head. Crouched by the fire,
we finally dried and Ma drove this time,
hand gripping the whip.
I know that Indian saved Pa's life,
and I know, too,
that Red Flower helped somehow.

"How much farther, Clem?" Ma asked weeks later.

"Soon, soon."

But Jenny and I wondered: did he know the way?

We'd heard tales of travelers lost for months.

Then we hit the drylands.

No trees, just prickly plants, rocks, and no good water.

We only drank once each day,

the oxen struggled to keep going,

and Red Flower's leaves curled up and dried.

"I'm thirsty, Pa!" Jenny complained.

"I know," Pa said, and bowed his head.

But Ma took a cup and trickled water

into Jenny's mouth and mine.

I swallowed some and spat a little

on Red Flower's soil. I told Jenny,

"If that flower dies, we'll never get to California."

Days later, I saw a small new leaf.

"We're going to make it!" Jenny cried.

Then the oxen threw their heads up, snorted,

and trotted toward some green trees.

Between was a small river,

and we splashed up to our knees.

Ma bathed Red Flower in the water and

I saw her lips moving, but I never knew—

was Ma praying or singing?

Then the nights began to cool. Pa said,
"Ahead are the Sierras—the last thing."
I was terrified when I saw those mountains
knifing the sky. The wagon tilted back,
the oxen snorted and pulled up one ridge,
down another, for days and days,
the oxen so weary we walked carrying packs.

I thought we'd *never* come to the end until one day
Pa locked the wheels for the final way down;
the wagon snaked and slid, faster and faster.
"Stand aside!" Pa yelled, chasing the oxen.
We ran after as Pa took a great leap,
hit the ox's legs, and brought the oxen to a stop.
"Are you all right, Clem?" Ma asked,
putting a shaking hand on his shoulder.
"All right, Rachel. How's your plant?"

We searched inside the jumbled wagon,

but could not find Red Flower.

Then Jenny lifted a pillow from the squashed plant.

"Here she is!"

Any other settler'd think us crazy,

patting that plant like it was an old dog.

But they didn't know what we did:

if something happened to Red Flower,

we would never get there.

At the foot of the mountains were the mining camps,

but Ma said, "Let's go north and find a peaceful spot."

Pa pursed his lips but agreed, and we journeyed

until we found a green meadow

stretched out like Ma's flowered calico.

Pa stopped the wagon and threw down his hat.

"California, here we are!"

Ma smiled and jumped down from the wagon

while Pa unhitched the oxen.

They ran and bellowed just like Jenny and me.

After Pa made a tent from the wagon cover and saplings,
Ma took out her shovel.
"Here's where my garden will be," she said.
"Jenny, James, bring me Red Flower."
Ma settled that tired old plant in the hole,
while I filled a bucket from the stream.
As the water trickled into the dirt,
I looked at Jenny—she looked at me.

We were like that red flower;
dug up from our home soil,
ferried over rivers, jolted over plains,
drylands, and killer mountains.
Ma drew us close in a hug so tight
I could not breathe.

She smiled then.

"Red flower will grow new leaves and buds.

And so will we, so will we."